This igloo book belongs to:

....

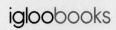

Published in 2014
by Igloo Books Ltd
Cottage Farm
Sywell
NN6 0BJ
www.igloobooks.com

HUN001 0514
6 8 10 9 7 5
ISBN: 978-1-78197-294-6

Printed and manufactured in China

Pirate's Treasure

igloobooks

"Ship ahoy, shipmate," cried Captain Bluebelly. "We've got treasure to steal." The crew of the Rotten Rose leaped into action and within minutes they were skimming across the ocean toward their target. Captain Bluebelly fired a cannon shot in front of the other ship's bow and the rest of the pirates pulled out their cutlasses. The Rotten Rose drew alongside the other ship and the pirates were just about to board, when there was an almighty crash.

All of the pirates, even Captain Bluebelly, were knocked to the deck. "What was that?" cried Bluebelly, as he scrambled to his feet. First Mate Barnacle rushed to the side of the ship and looked down at the water.
"Oops!" he cried. "We've crashed into a rock. There's a huge hole in our side and we're taking on water. It looks like we're going to sink if we don't get to dry land fast!"

"Ready about! Heave-ho!" bellowed Captain Bluebelly and the Rotten Rose did a quick turnaround and raced towards the nearest desert island. As they fled, they heard a loud shot and a cannonball ripped through their mainsail. The other ship had suddenly gotten brave when they realised that the pirates were retreating. Bluebelly swung around and shook his fist.
"Today's your lucky day," he yelled, "but next time we run into you, you won't be so lucky."

As they drifted towards land, another pirate ship appeared on the horizon. "Look," laughed its captain. "There's Captain Bluebelly and his cowardly crew running away from a bunch of softies. Perhaps we should call him Captain Yellowbelly from now on." He and his crew laughed so loud that the pirates on the Rotten Rose heard them and knew they were being laughed at.

The Rotten Rose just managed to make it to the desert island before the sail collapsed and water started to seep through the decking. Captain Bluebelly and Sam the Shipwright quickly surveyed the damage. "It don't look good, Cap'n," sighed Sam. "There's plenty of trees on the island for wood, but we're gonna need nails, rope, tar and cloth. It's gonna cost a fair bit. How much money have we got in the kitty?"

Captain Bluebelly turned a huge treasure chest upside down and gave it a good shake. The only thing that fell out was a rather angry spider. "Er, not a lot," replied Bluebelly. "It doesn't look like we'll be able to get the Rotten Rose back to sea. As if that's not bad enough, it looks like we're the laughing stock of the pirate world."

Sam would have liked to tell his captain that he was wrong, but at that very moment, a group of pirate ships were moored just offshore, roaring with laughter at the Rotten Rose and its crew.

Captain Bluebelly called a ship's meeting on the deck.
"Listen 'ere, shipmates. We've gotta make some cash — and fast,"
he explained. "Anyone got any ideas?"
"We could board a ship and seize some loot," said One-eye Jack.
"Er, the Rotten Rose ain't sailing anywhere," replied the captain.
"We could enter a sailing race and win some gold," said Simple Sid.

"I told you the Rotten Rose can't sail!" said Captain Bluebelly. While the rest of the crew scratched their heads and suggested more and more outlandish ideas, Titch the cabin boy leaned over the side and fished out a bottle he had seen floating by. There was something inside. Titch uncorked it and pulled out a sheet of paper. "Look at this," he cried, rushing to the Captain's side.

Captain Bluebelly squinted at the sheet of paper and then began to smile. "What we have here, Titch-lad, is a treasure map. It ain't just any old treasure map. It's Captain Cutthroat's treasure map." The crew of the Rotten Rose gasped. Every pirate worth his salt knew who Captain Cutthroat was.

He was the meanest pirate ever to sail the seven seas. He had died walking the plank without telling a soul where he had buried his hoard of treasure. "Head for shore!" cried Captain Bluebelly. "We've got Cutthroat's treasure to find."

The pirates crowded around Bluebelly on the beach. He began
to read the map. It started with a rock that looked like a seal.
"There it is," shouted Jim. All the pirates rushed over to it.
"Now take ten strides towards the crooked palm tree,"
said Bluebelly.
"One, two, three..." all the pirates counted the strides together.

Captain Bluebelly and his crew followed a winding path across the island, until they reached a gorge with lots of bridges going across it. Down below was a crocodile-infested river. "Which bridge should we take?" asked First Mate Barnacle. Captain Bluebelly looked carefully at each bridge. One bridge looked stronger than the rest.
"Let's try this one," shouted Bluebelly.

One by one, the pirates raced across the
rope bridge. Captain Bluebelly was the last
to go. He had almost made it to the other side,
when he heard the rope snap and found himself
dangling over the gorge. Sharp-toothed crocodiles
circled below him, but there was no way his crew
was going to allow him to become crocodile food.
Quick as a flash, they formed a human chain and
brought their captain to safety. "Phew! That was close,"
gasped Captain Bluebelly, "but let's keep going. We've got
treasure to find."

Captain Bluebelly was leading his crew along an overgrown path, when suddenly the ground gave way beneath his feet and he disappeared from sight.

"Where are you?" cried Sam.

"I'm down here. In some sort of pit. It's pitch black. Has anyone got a light?" shouted Bluebelly.

"Aye, aye, Cap'n," said Titch and he shone his lantern into the pit.

Suddenly, everybody began to yell. Captain Bluebelly had fallen into a pit full of writhing, hissing snakes. As one snake, with particularly long fangs, lurched at Bluebelly, Sam grabbed a vine and threw it into the pit. Without a second to spare, Bluebelly clambered to safety. As he panted beside the pit, his eyes caught sight of the crossed palm trees that marked the spot where Cutthroat's treasure was buried.

Quickly, the pirates pulled out the shovels they had brought with them and began to dig. Suddenly, Titch's shovel hit something hard. It was Captain Cutthroat's treasure chest. The crew of the Rotten Rose cheered as they heaved the chest out of the ground. They all gathered around as Captain Bluebelly opened the lid. Inside there was more gold and jewels than they'd ever seen. "Wow," gasped Captain Bluebelly.

"There's enough treasure here for us all to give up pirating and take up a life on dry land. What do you all think?" The crew of the Rotten Rose thought for a few moments and then all shook their heads. "Nah," said First Mate Barnacle. "We're all pirates through and through. Now let's get that ship fixed and put a stop to those other pirates laughing at us."

While Shipwright Sam and a team of willing helpers got to work sawing down trees to repair the Rotten Rose's hull, Captain Bluebelly and Titch rowed to the next island to buy the other supplies they needed. They had so much money that while they were ashore Captain Bluebelly and Titch decided to buy a new outfit for each of the pirates. The Captain was particularly pleased with his new hat.

Back on the desert island, there was much banging and sawing, patching and painting. Before long the Rotten Rose was shipshape once more. In fact, she looked so smart that Captain Bluebelly decided to rename her. "I rename you the Royal Rose," he cried, as he smashed a bottle over her bow and helped push her out to sea.

Captain Bluebelly and his crew no longer boarded other ships to fight the crew and steal their gold. Instead, they sailed the oceans in search of buried treasure. Once they found it, they would board other ships and divide the treasure among the poorest sailors.

They enjoyed their work so much that they were the jolliest pirate crew ever to sail the seven seas.